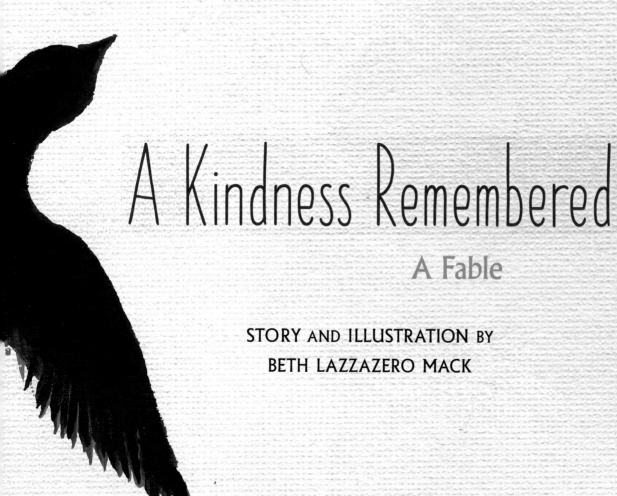

A Kindness Remembered

A Fable

STORY AND ILLUSTRATION BY
BETH LAZZAZERO MACK

The sun woke up
in its usual way.
It spread its dim light
on the start of the day.

The moon said goodbye
as it faded from sight for it
couldn't compete with the
sun's burning light.

2

3

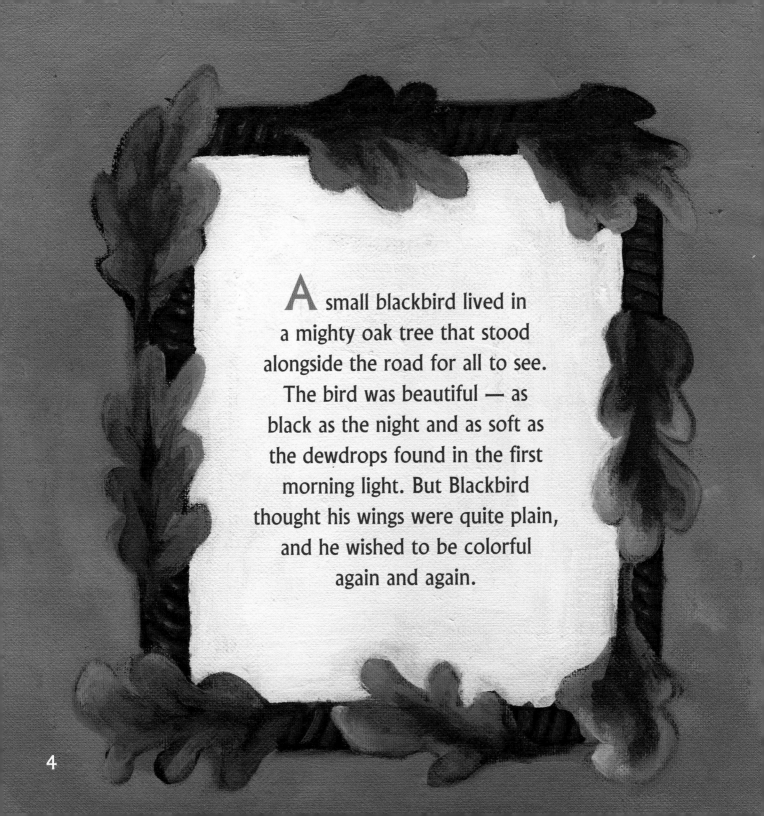

A small blackbird lived in
a mighty oak tree that stood
alongside the road for all to see.
The bird was beautiful — as
black as the night and as soft as
the dewdrops found in the first
morning light. But Blackbird
thought his wings were quite plain,
and he wished to be colorful
again and again.

4

5

"Yes," Blackbird thought, "Every evening at dusk when the sun goes down. It paints the sky and colors the town."

6

"If I go to the sun and fly my best,
perhaps I'll catch a sun ray
to pin on my chest."

He kissed his bird wife
and his fledglings, all three,
and chirped goodbye
as he flew from his tree.

He flew up to the clouds
as if in a trance
and failed to notice
the tip of a branch.

Blackbird spun and sailed
out of control,
landing head first
on a gravel road.

One wing was broken,
and he started to groan,
for he had a pain that hurt
right to the bone.

He looked up.
He looked down.
He looked all around.

Was there no one to help
a poor bird on the ground?

A peddler soon passed the bird's way.
He had a tan mare and sold pans and some trays.

"Please help me, kind sir,"
Blackbird chirped from the ground.
"I'm hurt and can't fly home to be safe and sound."

13

But the man was too busy
to care about this calamity
or that Blackbird might
miss his family.

"I hope somebody helps you,
poor mate," the man said.
"But if I stop now,
I'll be late, late, late!"

He was off
to market
so he set the bird
on a post, then
disappeared quickly,
just like a ghost.

15

The bird saw another traveler
at noon. This time it was a lady
eating cake with a spoon.

"Please help me," cried Blackbird again.
"I've been waiting so long in search of a friend."

17

18

But the proud woman
looked away and frowned.

She disliked the thought of feathers
on her brand new gown.

"There ought to be a law
against such laying about!"

Then she turned on her heel
and left with a pout.

Blackbird began to feel weary.
The sunset made his prospects look dreary.

The bird had nearly abandoned all hope when
one last traveler came down the road.

It was a very small boy,
ragged and cold.

"Poor little bird.
You are hungry and
hurt," the boy said.
"Would you like to share
a piece of my bread."

Then the boy wrapped him up
and took him straight home,
gave him some broth and brought
warmth back to his bones.

The boy and his parents cared for their friend until Blackbird's wing began to mend.

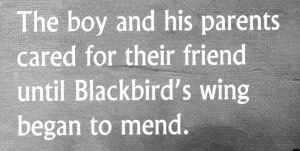

The bird said, "Now I must fly to my home in the wood. My wing has healed because of your good."

They set Blackbird free,
and he soared high in the sky.
He flew higher than any winged
creature had ever dared fly.

25

The tired sun stretched out its sleepy head
and turned the world yellow, orange, and red.

26

Blackbird spoke from the sky he so treasured:
"Farewell my friends!
Your kindness will always be remembered."

No longer longing for a new set of wings,
Blackbird settled in for a good night's sleep.

He closed his eyes and dreamed of the
new friends he would keep.

When the sun rose,
Blackbird's family gathered 'round.
His black wings had transformed
from the kindness he'd found.

Now whenever you see a blackbird
with sun-kissed wings, know he holds
kindness in his feathers and the
hope that sunrise brings.

Remember the red-winged blackbird
when you see a soul in need.

Even a small bird can be changed
by a good deed.

The End

Published by CrissCross AppleSauce,
A City of Light Publishing Imprint

www.CityofLightPublishing.com
266 Elmwood Ave., Suite 407
Buffalo, New York 14222

ISBN: 978-1-942483-52-6 (Softcover)
ISBN: 978-1-942483-53-3 (Hardcover)

Library of Congress control number
available upon request.

Printed in South Korea by Four
Colour Print Group - March 2020
Batch# 85882